BOREALIS

the DAY i I swapped my DAD for two 2 goldfisH

words by
neil gaiman

pictures by
dave mckean

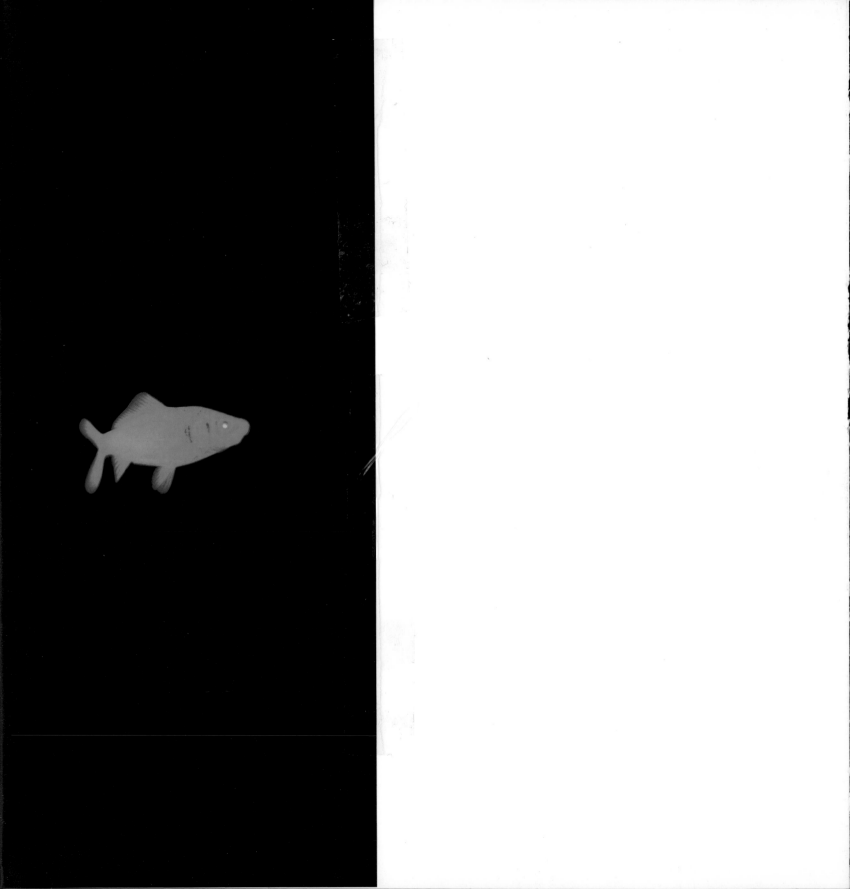

RIVER

Borealis is an imprint
of White Wolf Publishing.

White Wolf Publishing
780 Park North Boulevard, Suite 100
Clarkston, GA 30021
USA
World Wide Web Page: www.white-wolf.com

Book design by Dave McKean @ Hourglass

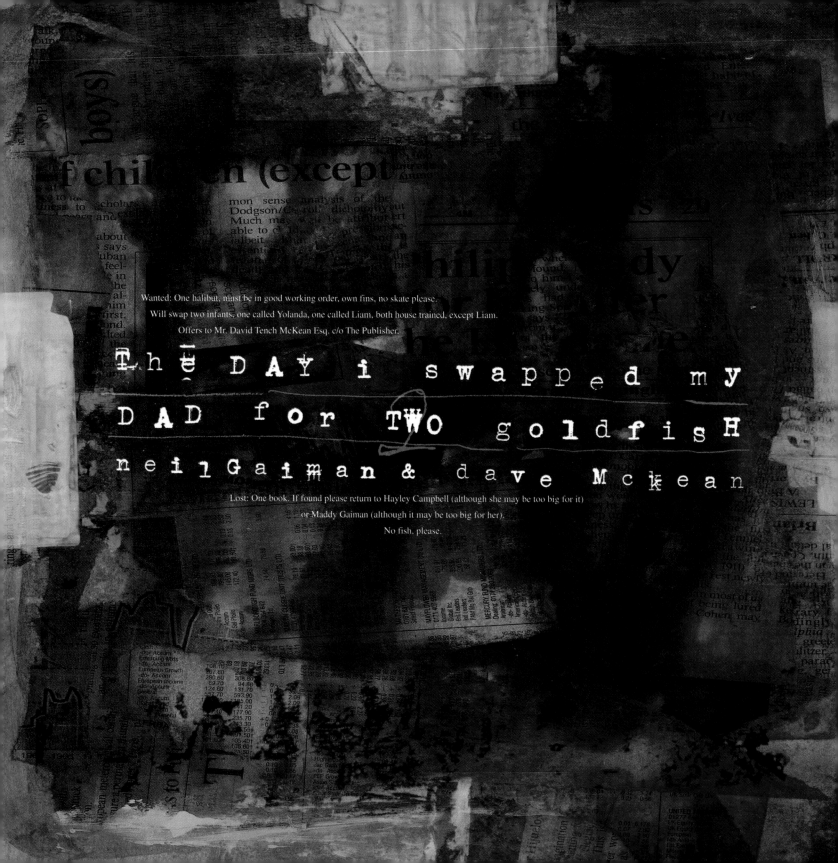

Wanted: One halibut, must be in good working order, own fins, no skate please.

Will swap two infants, one called Yolanda, one called Liam, both house trained, except Liam.

Offers to Mr. David Tench McKean Esq. c/o The Publisher.

The DAY i swapped my DAD for TWO goldfisH

neilGaiman & dave McKean

Lost: One book. If found please return to Hayley Campbell (although she may be too big for it) or Maddy Gaiman (although it may be too big for her).

No fish, please.

One day my mom went out and left me at home with just my little sister and my dad.

My dad sat in front of the television, reading his newspaper. My dad doesn't pay much attention to anything, when he's reading his newspaper.

They were pretty neat.

"I'll swap you them," I said.

"What for?" asked Nathan.

We went up to my bedroom.
My little sister tagged along.
I showed Nathan my old transformer
robots, and my baseball cards, and my books.
I showed him my old punching bag and my
penny whistle that Mommy said made her
head ache when I blew it. I showed him
my old spaceship that didn't float in the
bath any more, and the puppet with the
tangled strings, and I even showed him
Clownie, my clown that I sleep with.

I thought for a bit.

Some people have great ideas maybe once or twice in their life, and then they discover electricity or fire or outer space or something.
I mean, the kind of brilliant ideas that change the whole world.

Some people never have them at all.

When my mother came home I said, "Mom, can we buy some goldfish food?"

My little sister pointed at me.
He swapped him to his friend Nathan for those two goldfish.

My mother looked at me sharply.

"Right", said my mother, and she picked up the bowl of goldfish and handed it to me. "You can take these goldfish over to Nathan this minute, and don't you come back without your father."

"I told you so," said my little sister.

"And you can go with him," said my mother. "Fancy allowing your brother to swap your father for two goldfish and a bowl. The very idea."

So we went to Nathan's house.
He only lives over the road.
I knocked on the door.

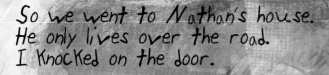

Nathan's mother came out.

Is Nathan here? I asked.

"Where did you get those goldfish," she asked me.

"They were a present to Nathan from his Aunt Violet."

"I swapped them," I said. "And now I have to swap them back again."

We went upstairs to Nathan's bedroom. It was even messier than my bedroom. Nathan had an electric guitar, a big white one.

Nathan,
I said to him,
What did you swap to Vashti, so she would give you her electric guitar?
If you get off me I will tell you,
he said.
I got off him.

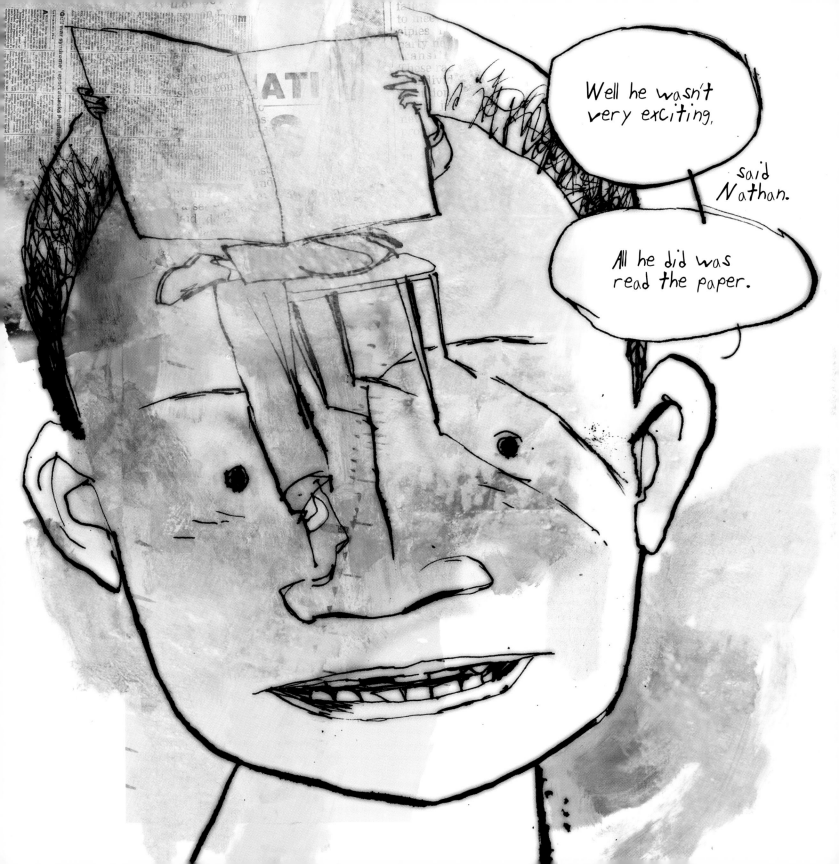

I rang Vashti's doorbell.
I've got your guitar for you.
I said to Vashti.
Vashti giggled.
All Vashti's sisters giggled too.
Can I have my dad back, please?
They giggled again.
Please Vashti,
said my little sister.
Vashti shrugged her shoulders.
Wait here,
she said.
She took the guitar away from me.

I put on the gorilla mask.
My sister went over to a policeman.
Help! QUICK!
shouted my sister.
That gorilla is escaping from the zoo!

Hee hee,
said my sister.
Watch it,
I told her.
Just watch it, that's all.

Blinky had a very big house.
We went up to the front and rang the bell.

Blinky came down the big stairs.
He looked very pleased to see the
gorilla mask.

"Are you bringing
it back?" he asked.

"Yes we are,"
I told him.

Blinky made the butler
give us ginger beer.

I liked it even though
the bubbles tickled
my nose.

My sister
made a face.

"Now," I asked,
when I finished
the ginger beer,
"Where's my dad?"

"Ah," said Blinky.
He went away again,
around the side
of the house.

I gave him the gorilla mask. He gave me Galveston
and a map he drew of how to get to Patti's house.

CONKERS

BIG SIGN
I'VE
GONE THE
WRONG
WAY.

LONG
WIGGLY
BIT

SIGN
POST

I'd never walked so far in my whole life.

While we walked, Galveston the Rabbit sat in my arms and made its nose go woffly. My sister tried to make her nose go as woffly as Galveston's but she couldn't do it.

They took the rabbit away from us and fussed over it, and gave it some lettuce.
Patti took my hand
Thank you for bringing Galveston back,
she said.
"We missed it".
We walked into the back garden.

There was a little rabbit hutch there,
and next to the rabbit hutch was a little
run with chicken wire all around it.
My dad sat on the grass, in the chicken wire run,
reading his newspaper and eating a carrot.
He looked a bit lonely, and he had grass all
over his trousers.

Last week my little sister told everyone at school that I was adopted. The week before she told everyone at school that I was a space alien pretending to be me.

When we got home my mother said things like, "Just look at the state of him!" and she made him go and have a bath and she put all his clothes into the washing.

While dad was in the bath, my mother told me off.

And when she'd finished
telling me off she made
me promise, cross-my-
heart, that I would
never - ever - swap
my dad for anything
ever ever again.

And I promised.

So I won't.

But I never promised anything
about my little sister...